To: Carol

Thank-you for being such a beautiful woman !!

# Controversial Poetry

*ADHD, A True Sickness*

Sara L. Wilson

authorHOUSE®

*AuthorHouse™*
*1663 Liberty Drive*
*Bloomington, IN 47403*
*www.authorhouse.com*
*Phone: 1 (800) 839-8640*

*Published by AuthorHouse 02/13/2018*

*ISBN: 978-1-5462-2841-7 (sc)*
*ISBN: 978-1-5462-2840-0 (hc)*
*ISBN: 978-1-5462-2908-7 (e)*

*Library of Congress Control Number: 2018901658*

*Print information available on the last page.*

# Contents

Dedication .................................................................................ix
Introduction ...............................................................................xi

Home—Free ................................................................................1
Labeled .....................................................................................6
Here's to the Life .........................................................................9
You..........................................................................................13
A Child's Night...........................................................................17
Tick .........................................................................................22
Sadness.....................................................................................26
A Teenage Boy ...........................................................................30
Hiding ......................................................................................33
Take Away This Pain....................................................................36
No One......................................................................................40
Fire, Fire....................................................................................43
Roses........................................................................................48
Overcome...................................................................................52
Mystic Beauty ............................................................................56
I'm Sorry....................................................................................59
Cherish Me ................................................................................64
Guardian Angel...........................................................................69
If Today ....................................................................................73
Reality.......................................................................................77
Going to Sleep............................................................................81
Hello, Sadness ...........................................................................85

Try and Find Me ................................................... 90
Alone ................................................................. 93
Would You Still Love Me? ...................................... 96
Grandma's Got a Gun ............................................ 99
A Funeral For My Best Friend ............................... 102
Going on a Trip .................................................. 107
Sociopath, Too Far Gone ...................................... 112
In a Dream ........................................................ 121
Why Won't You? .................................................. 123
Can't You See? .................................................... 126
Suicide .............................................................. 130
Garden .............................................................. 135
How Can You? .................................................... 138
On My Own ....................................................... 141
Invisible ............................................................ 146
Apart from Everyone ........................................... 151
Saddest Song ..................................................... 154
Smiles ............................................................... 157
I Just Want to Run .............................................. 160
Hello Darkness ................................................... 163
Hidden .............................................................. 167
Purpose ............................................................. 170
Payday .............................................................. 173
The Shadow ....................................................... 176
Shut ................................................................. 179
The Real Me ....................................................... 182
Twisted ............................................................. 185
The Cliff ............................................................ 188
On the Floor I Cry .............................................. 191
Guilty ............................................................... 194
No One Else ....................................................... 197
Bully ................................................................ 200
Life .................................................................. 203
Empty .............................................................. 206
Gravesight ......................................................... 210

Un-Chanced ...................................................213
You Took My Hand ..........................................216
You've Got that Somethin'..................................219
I Can't Understand...........................................221

About the Author.............................................225

# Dedication

Dedicated to:

*The Dead*

Gina Marie Lindberg—You will always be my bestie.
Kyle Hutchinson
Grandpa Art
Betty
Uncle Willie
Cousin Twyla
Clinger—Best male best cat ever.
Missy—Best female cat ever.
Raphael—Coolest hamster

*The Living*

Mom, Dad, Brother Mike

All my aunties, uncles, cousins, and grandparents: All of you are part of who I am.

All my friends: Throughout the years, you have always been remembered in my heart. Thank you for being part of my life.

Special thanks to:

Terry Johnson, Elli Banks, and the AuthorHouse team for being such wonderful people to work with. This book would not have been as amazing without your help.

Verona Pesti for allowing me to use some of Kyle's artwork. One of Kyle's dreams before passing away was to share his art with the world.

Sherry and Laverne Lindberg for your support, encouragement, thoughts, and input in the making of this book.

To my Bestie. I know you helped me get going on working on this book. You were a pure soul, and you are still felt here today. I will always cherish the times we had together, and one day I will be side by side with you again. I'll always remember your smile, your laugh, the way you lit up the room with your personality. The way you knew people and how you brought people together. You really did share Love with the world. At least I'll always have you as an Angel. Until I see you again my friend.

# Introduction

To my awesome family: Please know that you gave me the best life possible! The poems in this book express the mind of an ADHD child and the life experiences growing up. Some stories may be scary or hard to read. Please know that I had two awesome parents and the bestest big brother ever! There is no manual on how to raise children, let alone how to raise one who has a mental disorder, no matter the diagnosis.

Some stories were whipped up by my mind. Some were initiated by a book, TV show, story, dream, or random event. Not all poems were written to express my personal point of view; some try to express what someone else would feel or go through.

The artwork is provided by Kyle Hutchinson, who lost his battle to schizophrenia.

# Home—Free

School bell rings,
And I'm the last to leave
Because I know
What's going to happen to me.

They're going to call me names
And make me bleed from my face.
And then they will laugh
Because they think it's a race.

To home—free,
To home—free,
Where I am protected.
They can't hurt me.

Mom and Dad,
They don't know
I've crept down the hall
And heard their sorrow.

I've heard the words
That they have said,
And I take them with me
As I go back to bed.

To home—free,
To home—free,
Where I am protected.
They can't hurt me.

Alarm clock rings,
And I get ready.
As I slip from the covers,
I say goodbye to my teddy.

You're my only friend,
I will say to him.
I only feel safe
When wrapped in my arms you're in.

You keep me protected.
You never hurt me.
You keep me protected.
You're my home—free.

School bell rings,
And I'm the last to leave
Because I know
What's going to happen to me.

Mom and Dad,
They don't know
I've crept down the hall
And heard all their sorrow.

Oh, sweet teddy,
I'm glad you're here.
You know all my secrets
And soak up my tears.

You're my home—free,
You're my home—free.
You keep me protected.
You'll never hurt me.

## Side Note

This poem was written to express how I felt going to Dundonald School in Saskatchewan. I used to walk over to what I called the "Red School" at recess and lunchtimes—when I wasn't in detention, of course.

After spending a year at Confederation Park School, a school that teaches speech therapy to kids with ADD/ADHD and I'm sure other disorders, I went back to my old school.

I once again was picked on and made to feel that I was no good. From the devil.

I honestly don't think I would have made it one more year there.

Luckily for me, my dad got transferred back to Alberta. My poor big brother had to start junior high in a totally different province. I felt that I had just won the lottery! I was going to start a whole new school, where no one knew me, and I wore no label. I was a blank page.

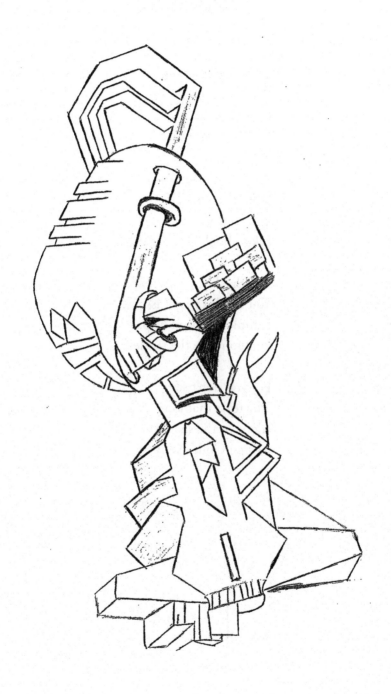

# Labeled

You say you see me;
You know who I am.
I say bullshit.
I mean, who can?

For I'm still finding
Who I am myself.
You look at me
Like a book on your shelf.

You think you can read me.
You think I've got issues.
I think you need help.
You don't see the tissues.

For you don't see
The tears that I cry
Alone in the shadows,
Asking God, "Why?"

## Side Note

On my report cards, all the teachers documented were my reactions when kids picked on me. "Sara does not get along well with others," the report would say.

If little Suzie ruined my picture or broke my crayons, my solution with the ADHD would be to punch her in the face. If little Timmy hit me with spitballs, I would lose it and throw my desk.

It was never put in the reports that I never colored on someone else's picture. I never went over and pulled someone else's hair. I never hit another kid with spitballs. I wasn't a bad kid. How I reacted was bad, but I wasn't a bad kid. They totally missed that part in their reports.

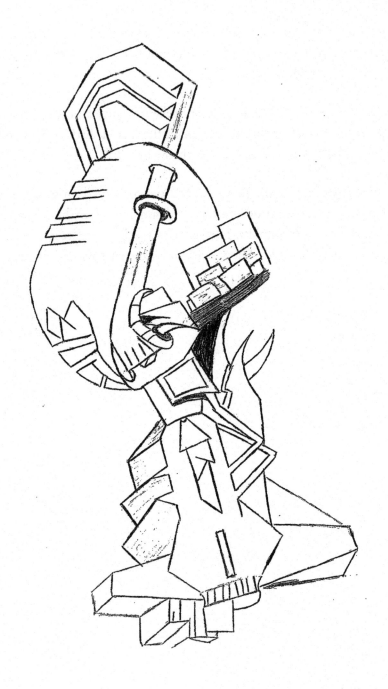

# Here's to the Life

Kicking and screaming,
But you do not care.
A tortured life
You've brought to share.
Amid the pain
And misery,
Here's to the life
You've given me.

Happy now
You're not alone.
Entwined in darkness
For you have not shown
What's beyond
This freezing cell.
You had me fooled;
I thought I was in hell.

Cuffed in chains,
I cannot leave.
What shall ever become
Of this soul in me?
You are sick,
Can't they see?
Here's to the life
You've given me.

You cannot get rid
Of pain with slaughter.
And you cannot wash away
Blood with water.
How did you expect
To be a parent
When you can look right through
Something that's not transparent?

Kicking and screaming,
But you do not care.
A tortured life
You've brought to share.
Amid the pain
And misery,
Here's to the life
You've given me.

## Side Note

As mentioned earlier, there is no manual on how to raise a child with mental illness. Even through all the love, the perceptions of an estranged mind are powerful.

As a child, I sometimes hated the fact that I was born. If I had the choice of being on earth or not, I would have chosen not.

I hated the feeling of fighting with myself, of trying to not become the label of ADHD. But then you're fighting against a part of you that is you.

# You

Hear my voice,
And hear it well.
You're my monster.
You're my hell.
You're a disease
That's in every cell.
You've seeped into my blood,
And now I don't feel well.

You're the demon
That's in my head.
You've turned dreams
To nightmares instead.
I scream, I scream,
I scream again still.
Hot and sweating,
You're making me ill.

You're my sickness.
You're my curse.
When I try to feel better,
I only feel worse.
Help me, help me
For I feel
That pretty soon, this world
Will no longer be real.

You're keeping me silent.
You're keeping me sound.
You're keeping my soul
Below the ground.
You're the cross
Above my grave.
You're the murderer
Who claims to save.

## Side Note

Being in a bad relationship doesn't help with the mean voices in your head.

Just because you're crazy and the others are "sane" doesn't mean that what they say is right, and everything you say is wrong.

You need to find someone who accepts you as you are and doesn't try to put you down in your moments of "craziness."

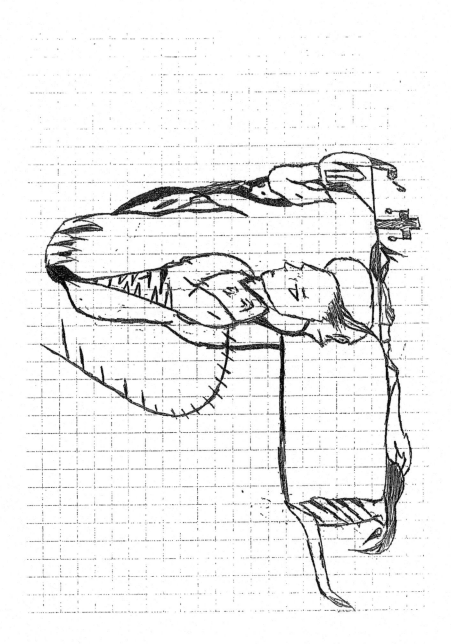

# A Child's Night

Monsters,
Monsters
In my head.
Running,
Running
Around my bed.
Sleep,
Sleep,
Begin to dream.
Nightmares,
Nightmares,
Making me scream.

## Side Note

Sometimes dreaming can be more exhausting than being awake. It used to feel like things were waiting for me to fall asleep to attack me.

I remember as a child dreaming of a lizard-like creature. He would take me to his cave. I had other repetitive dreams as well, but I remember specific nightmares of a lizard-like creature and his cave.

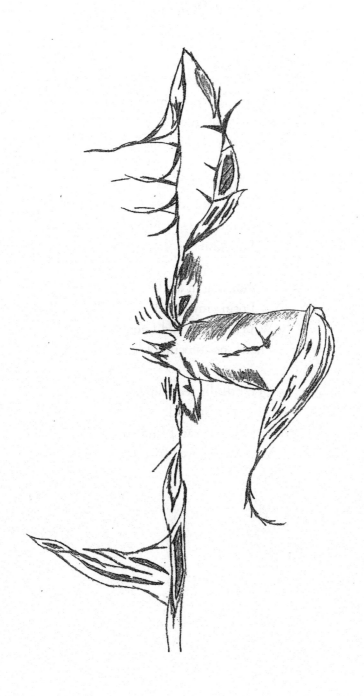

# Tick

The clock ticks by
The minutes in my life
That continue to go
On without you.

The clock ticks.
Every second I feel
My stomach is turning.
I'm gonna be sick.

Running in circles,
Losing my breath.
Which way should I go?
There's no direction left.

Frantically searching
For the end.
Tell me, where can I find you,
My dear, beloved friend?

## Side Note

I wrote this years before losing my best friend in a tragic car accident. I wrote this before experiencing any real loss. This poem didn't make sense to my life until after the death of Gina Marie Lindberg. Born June 18, 1986, she passed away September 20, 2014. She was twenty-eight years old and was just starting life with Keith Heaton. I really thought I was going to be a bridesmaid in her wedding. That's forever going to be an experience I wish I could have had.

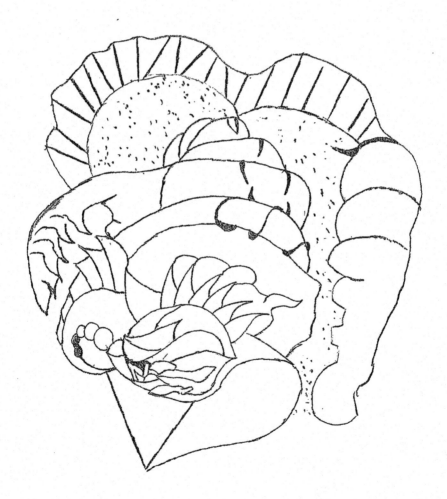

Kyle HooksLawson

24

# Sadness

In an endless well of darkness,
Unable to find my way out,
My screams echo in my head
As thunder and lightning shout.

Rain falling upon me,
Tears streaming down my face.
Heart pounding rapidly;
Against itself it will race.

For I am all alone,
Surrounded by shadows and fears.
Only sadness comforts me
As I cry with the sky's own tears.

And I begin to remember
About a time long ago,
Where sadness was replaced with anger,
With endless room to roam.

I was just a little girl,
With emotions I could not understand.
The reason for my existence,
This answer I tried to demand.

But I was only answered with silence.
Was told I came from the devil.
Words deterred me from God.
Was placed in the emptiness I lay in.

## Side Note

After being mad and fighting for so long, I was exhausted. That's when the feeling of being defeated and sad crept in and took over.

My anger episodes had teachers saying mean things about me. Maybe they didn't know that their words echoed in my screaming head for years after.

Kids remember when they are told they are "no good," "worthless," and asked, "What's wrong with you?" Even after days and nights, good times at the amusement park, when they lay their little heads on their pillows at night, those bad words keep coming back to haunt them.

# A Teenage Boy

Dark hair,
Blue eyes,
With a soul the size of an ocean
Deep inside.

Divine beauty
Could not describe
How in one heart,
So much passion could lie.

Long lashes,
Strong hands,
With the energy of a boy,
But what you see is a man.

Calm waters that show,
With rapids under way.
With life in its sea,
Finding its way each day.

## Side Note

When those teenage years came, all it would take was one look from a boy to make me sigh.

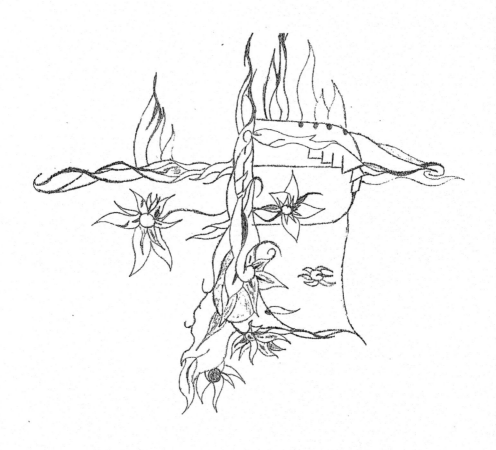

# Hiding

You're right there,
Yet you're not
Here
Beside me.
You're so far away.
I wish I could make you stay
For real.
Your arms I need to feel
Around
Me tightly
While you touch my body lightly.
And your lips,
How you kiss.
I hate
How you can make me miss.
Why can't you see
How great we've made reality
While you stand right in front of me.
You hide.
There's something inside
That you're scared I'm gonna find.
But what could it be?
How can you hide from destiny?

## Side Note

When someone keeps himself or herself from you, when normally it's the other way around.

# Take Away This Pain

Screaming,
Screaming.
Can't you hear me?
Naked,
Naked.
Can't you see me?
On my knees,
Begging God to please
Take away this pain.

## Side Note

When the mental illness has taken you to your breaking point.

# No One

No one wants to talk to me.
No one wants to be my friend.
I'm left alone
In a world of pretend.

Don't pay attention
If you're just gonna be mean.
Don't mind me.
I just have to scream.

Alone.
Alone
Is better than
The pain
And hurt
You're making me feelin'.

Turn off the lights;
It hurts my eyes.
Just walk away.
Don't hear my cries.

Footsteps.
Footsteps
Down the hall.
No one cares.
No one at all.

## Side Note

Early elementary is tough on any kid. But once they knew they could break my crayons and watch me freak out about it, that's when things got really rough. Especially when I was the only one in detention for it.

Mom and Dad read me stories and tucked me in bed. While they were showing me love, all I wanted was to be alone with my screaming thoughts. But then once I was alone, I didn't want to be anymore.

# Fire, Fire

Fire, fire
All around.
The heat is burning.
I scream out loud,
But no one hears.
My burning flesh
Is bubbling and sizzling
Along my chest.

Fire, fire,
Burning within.
It's melting my knees
Into my skin.
My eyes are popping
Out of their sockets.
You have the power.
Oh, won't you stop it?

Save me, save me.
Don't you care?
Help me please.
How can you stare?
Is it fun
To watch me die,
To watch me burn
With fire inside?

Revenge, revenge
Would taste so sweet.
To feel the pain
That's gone through me.

Fire, fire,
Make it burn.
I laugh out loud
As it's your turn.
No one hears
Your monstrous screams,
And I won't save
Who wouldn't save me.

## Side Note

So many times, other kids created a circle around me and "watched the show." I wished they could feel what I was feeling when I had no control of my brain freak-outs. Maybe then they wouldn't be so mean.

# Roses

Roses, roses
On my grave.
Another funeral.
It's all the same.
People come,
And then they leave.
A single tombstone
To represent me.
Was I real?
Who was I?
Was I worth
A day to cry?
Was I worth
A day to celebrate
And a night to remember?
Beyond this gate
May this soul
Be laid to rest.
But I still live.
I can't just let
My soul to die
Without at least
Knowing why
I lived as me.

Anyway, now I lay
Buried beneath
All this dirt.
I must be alive
For I still hurt.
I'm alive.
Please unbury me.
I'm alive.
Please release me.
I'm still alive.

## Side Note

Just one of those moments when you think what your funeral would be like, And then you start thinking about how freaky it would be to be buried alive.

Not sure if this is the reason, or the fact that I am terrified of creepy, crawly insects, but I would like to be cremated when I die.

# Overcome

Why am I going through this?
Tell me what have I done.
I look up to the sky,
And I try to overcome.

Blue sky,
White clouds,
Sun's rays
Warm me all around.

There's an energy inside,
One that I cannot control.
Its raging cries,
And I do not know why.

Why I am going through this?
Tell me what have I done.
I look up to the sky,
And I try to overcome.

## Side Note

As a hypersensitive kid with ADHD, I had little to no control of my emotions and felt things I could not explain.

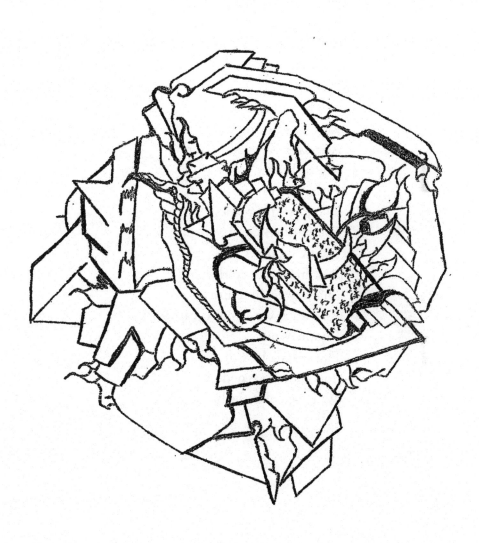

# Mystic Beauty

Mystic beauty,
Please don't cry.
Through your tears
I see the pain inside.
Mystic beauty,
You have the power.
Rise to the heavens,
And look over your tower.
Mystic beauty,
Please don't weep.
There's still happiness
You must still seek.
Mystic beauty,
Lost from your world,
One day you'll return
And teach what you've learned.
Mystic beauty,
Please don't be sad.
You know the good
Will overcome the bad.

## Side Note

When you imagine what it would be like to see an angel cry.

# I'm Sorry

I'm sorry that you can't see
What I've given up.
I'm sorry that I'll never be
Quite good enough.
I'm sorry that you won't give me
What it is I need.
I'm sorry, but I feel
That you're consumed with greed.

I look in your eyes,
And it looks like you're looking back.
But it seems you look right through me.
Because understanding you lack,
You use your words to hurt me.
You're the one on the attack.
So tell me, tell me,
Who's the maniac?

I'm sorry that you surpass
Everything that's good.
I'm sorry that I fail
At things you never would.
I'm sorry that I don't hear
The mumbled words you say.
I'm sorry for not speaking
Like it matters anyway.

I look to your eyes,
And it looks like you're looking back.
But it seems you look right through me.
Because understanding you lack,
You use your words to hurt me.
You're the one on the attack.
So tell me, tell me,
Who's the maniac?

## Side Note

A year turns into two, then three, then four. At about four and a half years, it hit me. I didn't want to imprison myself with a five-year to life sentence with someone.

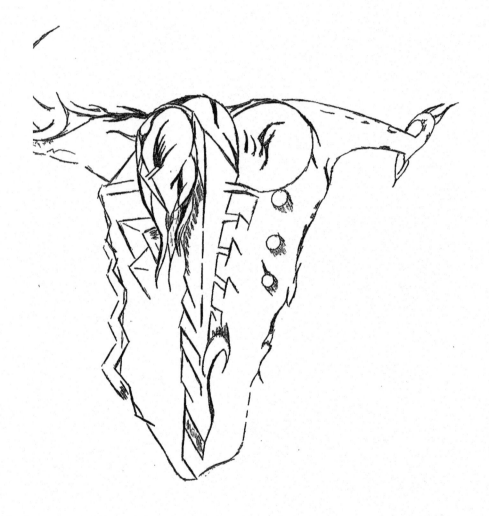

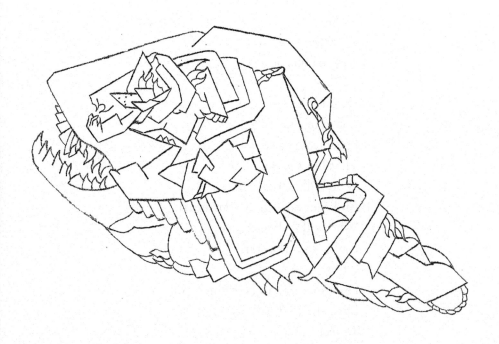

# Cherish Me

Cherish me.
Hold me in your arms at night,
Say to me
Everything will be all right.
Can't you see
How much I need you,
All the pain that I've gone through?
I just need you to try
To hold me close as I cry.

I need to let go.
I need to move on.
I need to be told
That I'm the only one
Who will feel your arms
And the warmth of your heart.
Who will feel your love
Right from the start
Of us.
I'm not trying to be righteous.
I just thought I deserved
To feel this
At some point in time.
Tell me that you will be mine.

To cherish
And hold,
To be kept warm,
Forgetting the cold
All through the night.
Everything will be all right
Because you'll forever be
Cherishing me.

## Side Note

To just be able to let go and jump face-first into love.

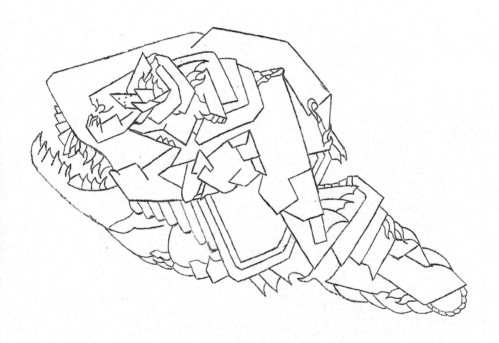

# Guardian Angel

Guardian angel,
Hear my prayer.
Hear my voice.
You must be somewhere.
Have you always
Stayed close by,
Or have you flown too far
To hear my cry?

Here are my tears
For they're for you.
My soul is lost
And wandering to
An unknown place.
And I'm not sure
I want to stay.

## Side Note

I know I have guardian angels. Even when I'm pushing myself away from them.

# If Today

If today were to be the end,
Tell me, have you really tried
To accomplish everything you could
And to live without a lie?
Have you been honest
Or consumed with greed?
Did you capture animals
Or set them free?
If someone needed
To let you know,
Could you keep a secret
Years past tomorrow?

## Side Note

A basic look at your life.

Kyle H

# Reality

All alone
In a world of unknown.
Can't be reality
For it can't be shown.
But is it just
Another form
Of planet earth
For when we're gone?

Reality.
Tell me, what does it mean?
Is it what's real?
At the time of our being,
You think you have won
With war and destruction.
Can't you see,
Or am I the only one?
You have a twisted version
Of reality.

# Side Note

Some people's perception of reality can be really scary.

# Going to Sleep

Going to sleep,
Fighting for life.
When I wake up,
Will I feel alive?
In my dreams,
It's like I'm really there.
I feel emotions,
And I'm well aware

That I might carry
This dream along with me
Into the real world
From a realm of fantasy.
I dream of struggling
And wake up tired.
I dream of demons.
It's like I'm wired

Into other worlds
That need to be saved.
I wake up on earth
And feel enraged.
I wake up screaming
Into a world of deceiving,
Lies, cheating,
Pain, and stealing.

Going to sleep.
It's never-ending,
Always suffering,
Always suffering.

## Side Note

As a child, I had crazy dreams and nightmares. Sometimes I couldn't tell which was worse: my nightmares or being awake.

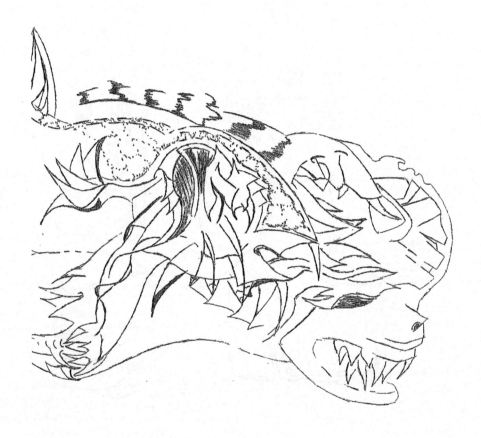

# Hello, Sadness

Hello, sadness.
Swallow me whole.
Engulfed in darkness,
With no room left to grow.

For I am dead inside,
And this is no lie.
If you only took the time
To look inside my eyes.

You would find nothing left
Inside, and realize
My whole life and its existence
Have been shrouded in clouds of lies.

Look in my eyes.

What color are they?
Cold and black.
They used to change with emotions,
But all feelings I now lack.
For I am dead inside,
And this is no lie.
If you only took the time
To look inside my eyes.

Even my heart has abandoned me.
Begone is my soul.
Even my passion is gone.
My own thoughts have left to roam.

Hello, sadness.
Swallow me whole.
Engulfed in darkness,
With no room left to grow.

## Side Note

When you have completely shut down, you wonder how much of a zombie you look like. Just an empty shell, trying to go through everyday life with such sadness in your eyes.

# Try and Find Me

Locked inside,
With chains on tight,
Try and find me
With all your might,
Hidden behind
These slimy walls.
Watch your step
For you may fall
Down a trap
You could not see
For it is dark
Where you need to find me.

## Side Note

When mental illness has sunk its clutches in you and dragged you to its dark cave. You have closed off and fallen into darkness. Trying to get back into the light is harder than it sounds.

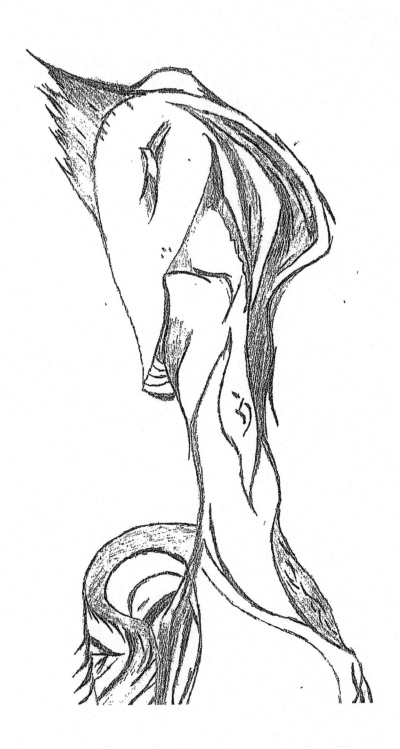

# Alone

How am I supposed to find
Arms like yours to wrap around my
Body and soul, so warm inside?
I'm so cold, so cold.

How is anyone supposed to see
The ocean's tide that runs through me?
You looked through my eyes and saw my destiny.
Now I'm blind.

I'm shaking.
So cold.
Can't see where I'm going.
Oh no.
I can't see you.
I can't feel you.
I'm alone.

How could anyone ever fulfill?
The love you gave, I feel it still.
I long for you against my will
For I'm so alone,
Shaking,
Cold,
Can't see.
Oh no.

Alone.

## Side Note

When your heart has been ripped out and shattered.

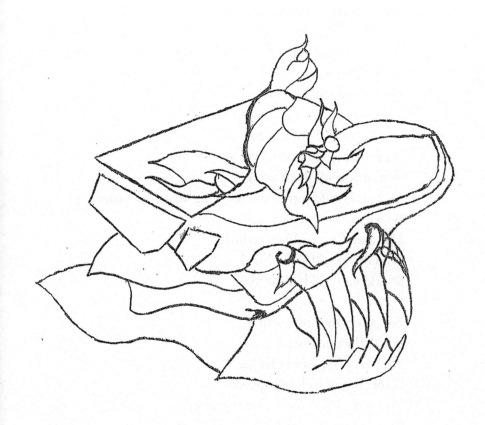

# Would You Still Love Me?

Would you still love me
Even if I told you a lie?
Would you still love me
Even if I broke down and cried?
Would you still love me
If you knew all about the pain I've kept inside?
Would you still love me?
Would you still love me?

Would you still look at me
With that look in your eyes and smile?
Would you still look at me
As if you could picture me walking down the aisle?
Would you still look at me
Like I make your life worthwhile?
Would you still look at me?
Would you still look at me?

For you're the one I want.
You're the one I need.
You're the one I can't let go.
Sometimes it feels like greed.
I want to share with you everything,
But there are things I can't let go.
I don't want to hide from you,
But there are things that you can't know.

Unless I know.
Would you still love me?
Would you still love me?

## Side Note

When you realize you've fallen in love with someone, but you're still crazy.

# Grandma's Got a Gun

Grandma's got a gun;
I guess she's come undone.
Don't dare ask for a cinnamon bun,
Grandma's got a gun.

Bang, bang
She shot them down.
When she – went into town
Bang, bang.

When she pulled the trigger,
Did the touch make her quiver?
Did her eyes even flicker?
When she pulled the trigger.

Now grandma's on the run.
Like hide and seek,
You can have some fun.
But when you get caught,
Don't get distraught.
Now grandma's on the run.

So grandma's gone for a ride.
Where do grandma's go to hide?
At barbor's, and bakery's,
Police go inside.
But grandma's gone for a ride.

## Side Note

A random story

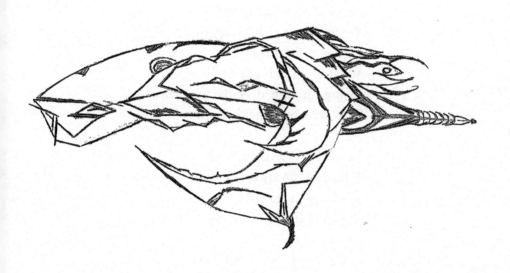

# A Funeral For My Best Friend

I can't believe you're dead.
A funeral for my best friend.
Black dress,
Tears pouring down.
I had a speech,
Can't remember what I said.

You were my best friend.
We went everywhere together.
Liquor and car rides,
What's two girls gonna do?
Going through all of the moments,
That we have gone through.

I can't believe you're dead.
A funeral for my best friend.
Walking on tea cups,
Enjoying the country.
The nice trees,
Gone now is your company.

You were my best friend.
We went everywhere together.
Which town were we in?
Where were we partyin'?
Fun times were everywhere.
Now you're not here.

I can't believe you're dead.
A funeral for my best friend.
Black dress
So much, and so little was said.
When will I see you again?
I miss you, my friend.

# Side Note

Gina Marie Lindberg

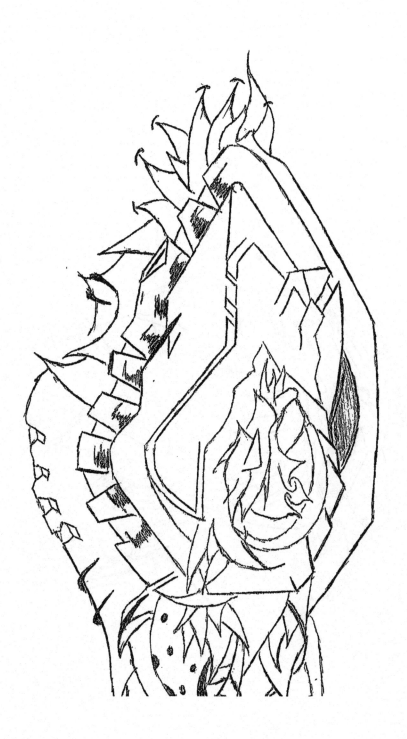

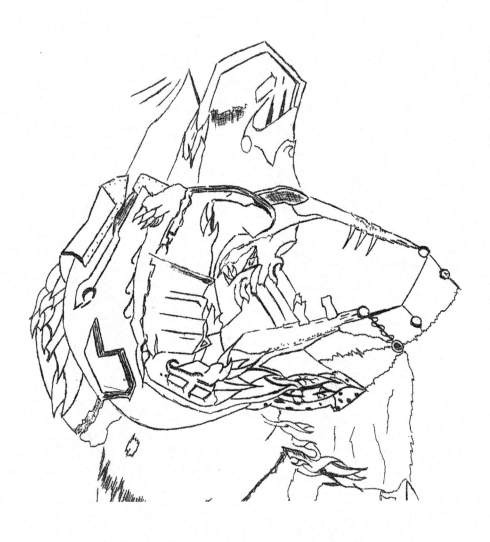

# Going on a Trip

Going on a trip.
Going to escape.
Going to run away from this world
For it is filled with hate.

Going on a one-way train.
Never coming back.
Finding a place filled not with pain,
A place where I can relax.

For I am tired of going nowhere,
And no one hearing my screams.
I am tired of being haunted
By what comes in my dreams.
I am tired of this illusion.
Nothing's as it seems.
I want to go and find the angels
And hear their songs and hymns.

I want to go and search,
And stop when I may find
A place of peace and harmony,
A place to rest my mind.
I know that there's gotta be
A place that's not like this.
A place opposite of this torture.
A world full of happiness and bliss.

Going on a trip.
Going to escape.
Going to run away from this world
For it is filled with hate.

Going on a one-way train.
Never coming back.
Finding a place filled not with pain,
A place where I can relax.

For I am tired of going nowhere,
And no one hearing my screams.
I am tired of being haunted
By what comes in my dreams.
I am tired of this illusion.
Nothing's as it seems.
I want to go and find the angels,
And hear their songs and hymns.

## Side Note

When you just want to run away to some place new, but you know you'll still have the same issues.

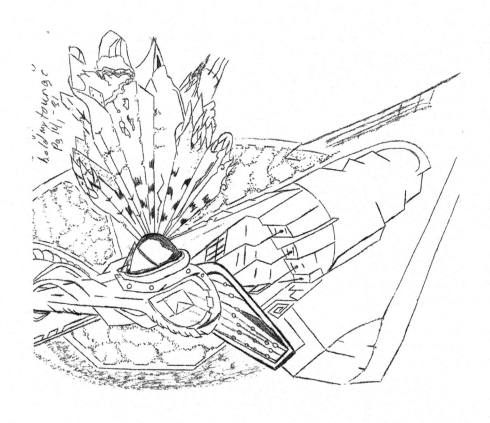

# Sociopath, Too Far Gone

So what if I'm a freak,
Walking with schizophrenia.
Maybe I'm bipolar,
And I'm walking up to ya.

I've got multiple personalities.
Take one look and run.
Tell me, which one do you see?
How far has my soul gone?

Into a sickness.
Where's a doctor?
Prescribe me some pills
That take me nowhere.

Tell me what's the cure
For an unbalanced mind?
Take a look inside my head,
And tell me what do you find?

## Side Note

It's hard when you've struggled with a mental illness, but when a friend is going through one, you don't know how to help.

The
dragon
Lays

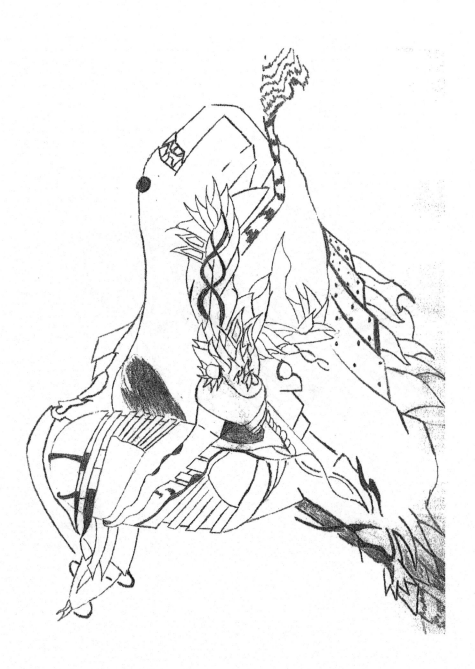

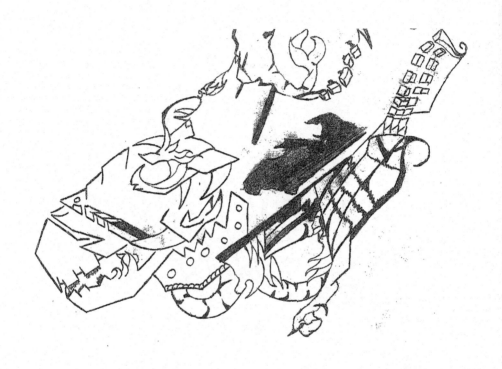

Kyle Hutchinson
AKA Killien switch

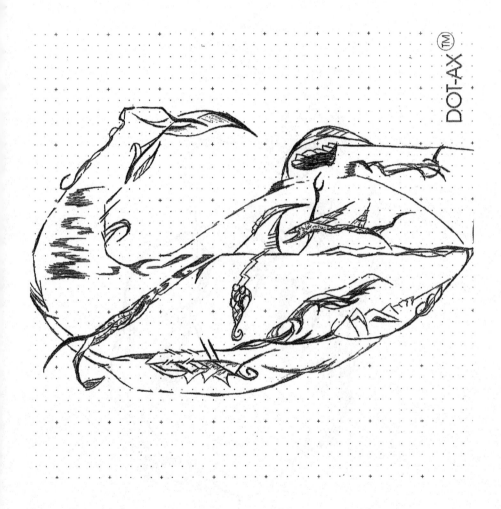

DOT-AX ™

# In a Dream

I look out the window.
There's a book lying on the branch of the tree.
I want to go get it.
That means going outside, and I might fall.
The old me would go for it.

I climb out the window
And walk on the roofed balcony.
There is a soft patch; it doesn't hold me.
I fall right through.
I go tumbling down
And land on the crumbled ruins.
There is something lying by my hand.
I think it's the book.
It's a dead mouse.
I wake up.

## Side Note

I had a lot of weird dreams.

# Why Won't You?

Why won't you just hold me?
Why won't you just be there for me?
Why do you expect me
Just to do things for you?
I'm needing things
That you won't give.
You expect me to live
Just for you.

A prisoner of life.
A prisoner of doom.
A prisoner of dreams.
A prisoner of you.
All I ever wanted
Was to have someone near.
All I ever desired
Was to share what I fear.

Why won't you just hold me?
Why won't you just be there for me?
Why do you expect me
Just to do things for you.

## Side Note

When you realize that you're in a one-way relationship.

To boot

# Can't You See?

Can't you see
We are still two strangers
With two separate pasts,
Feeling different in danger?

I still feel
That I'm still fighting
Something that's not real.
You might find it enlightening

To know what you're up against.
But you haven't shown
Whether you're playing dense,
Or you just don't want to know.

Sometimes I see two people.
I'm trying to learn who you really are.
Sometimes you're sweet; sometimes you're cruel.
Or has my mind gone too far?

## Side Note

Basically, when two people who are opposites are together and really shouldn't be.

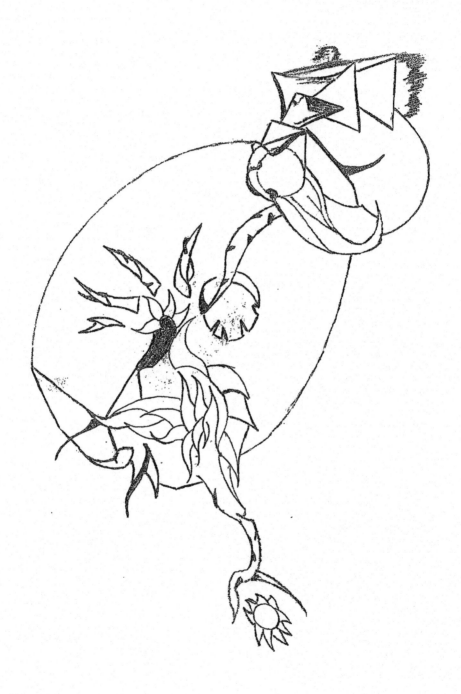

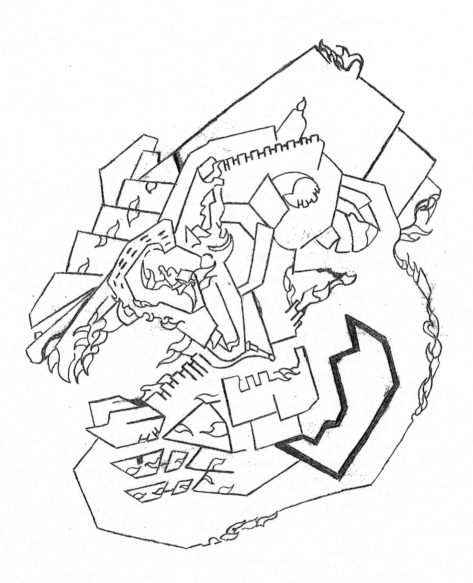

# Suicide

Suicide is called a sin,
While crucifixion allows life to begin.
We all look to you as God.
But I think of you as a coward
For on this earth you could not bear
How much we humans do not care.

How much pain we can cause before death.
How much blood can come from your breath.
Yet, we are told that we are to praise
The agony you suffered in just a few days.
Even you did not fight,
But you have many believing
With all their might

That you have power.
You're the God Almighty.
That's why you leave us here
To feel the agony.

So what if I
Were to sacrifice myself?
The pain I have gone through,
Has it not been enough?

The blood I have bled.
The tears I have shed.
Why won't you take me away
And make all this end?

So you are the one
They think of as great.
Let us praise
For this is the best you could create.

## Side Note

When you would rather be crucified and set free, instead of continuing to live in this world.

Kyle Hutchinson

# Garden

Walking in a garden.
Walking in a garden of graves.
Walking in a garden.
What's going to happen today?

What am I going to find?
Could I find the roses?
What am I going to see
Before the gate closes?

Locks me here forever?
Traps me here forever?
Tell me, what will I never
Ever see again?

Lying in a garden,
I think I've been here before.
Lying in the scent of roses,
It's dark; please close the door.

## Side Note

Has anyone else laid down in a graveyard?

# How Can You?

How can you
Expect me to see
When you keep me blinded
From my destiny?
You push me forward
While holding me back,
And then you question
How I choose to react.
You try to create
A life for me.
But it can't be real
When it wasn't supposed to be
Lived in such
A certain way,
Where I can't be free
To go about my day
And to bring my dreams
Into a world that you know.
But first I have to leave
In order for me to show.
For you could not understand
What all goes through my head.
And I cannot explain it,
So I will show you instead.

## Side Note

When you know as a child that you need to change the way you act, but you just want to be the way you are.

# On My Own

On my own.
Forever on my own.
I can't rely on you.
What can you do
To help me?
Help me.
I'm on my own.
No one can understand.
Could never understand.
No matter how much I scream
Or try to demand,
It will not come.
I will live my life
Just to have it come undone
With no one.
No one's there.
Why would anyone care
To look at me,
To hold me?
Why would anyone?
Why would you?
I'm on my own.
Forever on my own.
No one to lean on.
No one to carry me.
I guess I'm too heavy
For you to carry me.

I'm all alone.
No one to talk to.
With nothing to say,
Why would you listen?
Why would you even
Care about what I have to say?
So it doesn't matter.
It has never mattered
Because I'm all alone.
Left on my own.
I can't rely on you.
What can you do
To help me?
Help me.
I'm on my own.
No one can understand.
Could never understand.
No matter how much I scream
Or try to demand
For happiness,
It will not come.
I will live my life
Just to have it come undone.
Alone.
On my own.
I guess I'll forever be
On my own.

## Side Note

No matter how much love and friendships are around you, mental illness is a very lonely disease.

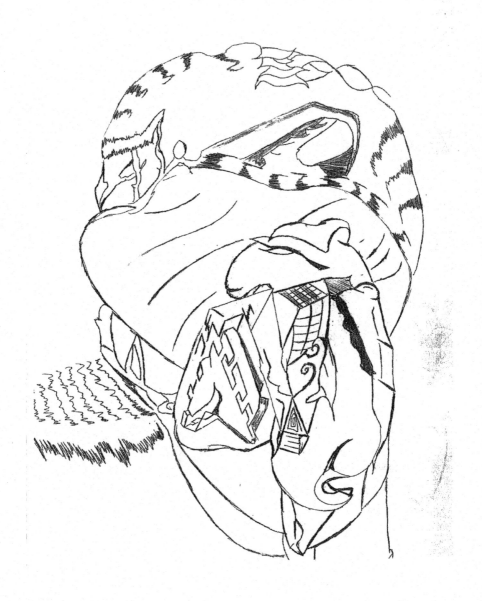

145

# Invisible

Some kind of invisible
One you can't see.
But I can feel pain,
And this pain shall set me free.

Look at me.
Look at me.
Tell me, what do you see?
Look at me.
Look at me.
How should I be?

You look right through
What you do not know.
But I can't leave.
I have nowhere to go.

Look at me.
Look at me.
Some kind of invisible
One that you can't see.
Tell me,
Tell me,
What should I be?

I am life.
I am death.
I'm the cold
That comes off your breath.

I'm the heat
That scorches your skin.
I'm the screams
That cry within.

Some kind of invisible
One that you can't see.
But I can feel pain,
And this pain shall set me free.

## Side Note

How can anyone help you with the demons that are inside your head?

# Apart from Everyone

Apart from everyone,
But I don't know why.
How can I be so different?
I, too, bleed and cry.

How can you be
So quick to discriminate?
You think you're superior
As you're filled with hate.

You kill love
And fill the world with pain.
But I'm the one you fear
And try to restrain.

Apart from everyone,
But I don't know why.
How can I be so different?
I, too, bleed and cry.

## Side Note

I didn't understand why I felt so different from the other kids.

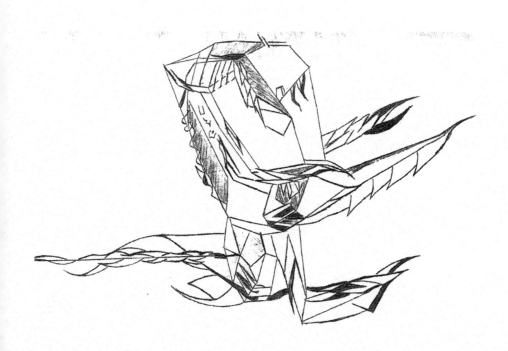

153

# Saddest Song

Feels like the saddest song.
Where do I go now,
With everything gone wrong?
And I don't know how
To continue to live
When every day
I just want to give
This saddest song away.

## Side Note

Depression is a disease that can creep up and take over at random.

# Smiles

She smiles through tears.
Can't release her fears
Unto a man
Who could never understand
Her hidden pain
That still remains
Inside her heart,
Tearing her apart.
What could he do
To heal the pain that she's gone through?
So she smiles.
She tries to forget
Her past life
And all the regret.

## Side Note

When you try to let go of the pain and hide in someone's arms.

# I Just Want to Run

I just want to run.
Go to places I want to be.
I just want to run.
See faces I want to see.
To learn not hatred
And the meaning of despair,
To meet new people
And live without a care.
To be on my own,
To run wild, to run free,
To be on my own,
Exploring my own journey.
To run and hide,
No one in front,
Left back,
Or by my side.
To find a new world
I didn't realize.
To follow my dreams
And find what I fantasize.

## Side Note

I used to wonder what it would be like to jump on a train and see where it took me.

# Hello Darkness

Hello darkness.
Bring me into your light,
Where I feel safe.
And I feel all right
In behind the shadows.
I'll let you see my soul.
I'll no longer hide.
I'll tell you everything you want to know.

Naked in front of you,
Blanketed in blackness.
Goodbye reality.
Hello to madness,
Where I can be strong,
And I can be sane
Because I feel nothing
From love to pain.

I've learned to find shelter.
I've learned how to hide.
But now I can't seem
To show my true feelings inside.
So only in darkness
Do I have the courage to show
My truth,
My lies,
And all I've kept unknown.
Because in behind my passion
Lies a hidden sorrow
That no matter how hard I tried,
I was destined to be alone.

## Side Note

Darkness. When it's the sunniest day but you still feel dark inside. When you're surrounded by people, but you still feel alone.

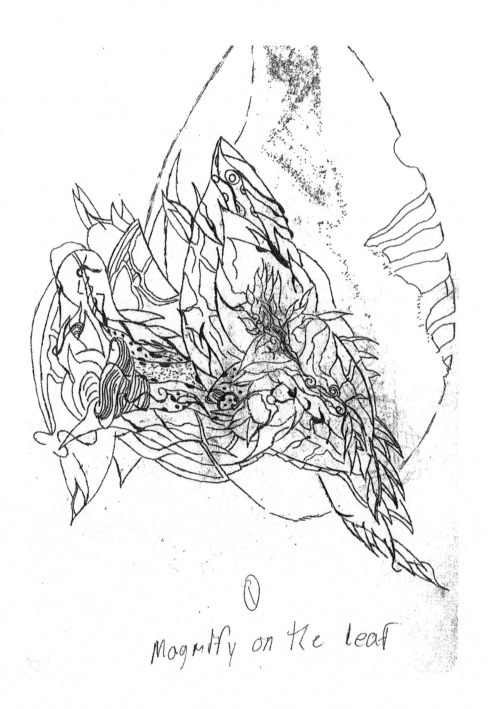

Magnify on the leaf

# Hidden

Eyes wide open,
And yet she cannot see.
With words inside her head,
She never dares to speak.
Even in dreams
She tries to run away.
But no matter where she goes,
It brings her to today.
Heart beating fast,
Yet her legs move slow.
Always in a hurry
But never wants to go.
Her cuts bleed,
Her wounds heal,
Never shedding a tear
Or showing how she feels.
She wants to hold him close
But always lets him go.
Keeping inside the secret
That he really should know.

## Side Note

How do you explain anxiousness? A teenage crush but too scared to make a move.

# Purpose

What is my purpose?
Why am I here?
With every new day that comes,
Comes another tear.
Feeling my hate.
Feeling my pain.
Don't know how long
I'll be able to restrain.

## Side Note

As a kid, I wondered if there was ever going to be more to me than just my ADHD.

172

# Payday

Today's payday,
And I'm going to the mall.
Going to buy a gun.
Going to shoot them all.
No questions.
No reasons why.
Hearing your screams
As you die.
You might as well
Consider yourself dead.
The next time I see you,
It's going to be the end.

## Side Note

People should not have guns. What do you think they're going to do with that gun? Hearing about all the guns in the United States, how many of the owners have a mental illness? People do snap. I'm not saying it's right, but I can understand how teens, moms, and dads reach their limits and resort to guns to end the madness. I don't believe in guns.

# The Shadow

I go to you to comfort me, to make me
understand, and to get me to see.
I had gotten to believe that you would be there forever, for all eternity.
It came as a surprise.
But when you were not there, I could finally realize
That you were just a dream, just a myth to wake up with
doubt in my mind to believe in a passing shadow.
If it would have only stopped to open up,
It could have become a part of you.
But closing and darkening itself
is what makes it the black and haunting figure passing by.
There are no reasons
Or explanations.
It absorbs you, knows you, and takes a part of you away,
Leaving you with a pain of helplessness.
It hurts but does not care, which is why it is now gone.
Only you are left
To become stronger than you could have ever been before.

## Side Note

When you're in love, but he's the one who's scared and runs away. I wrote this one in grade 7.

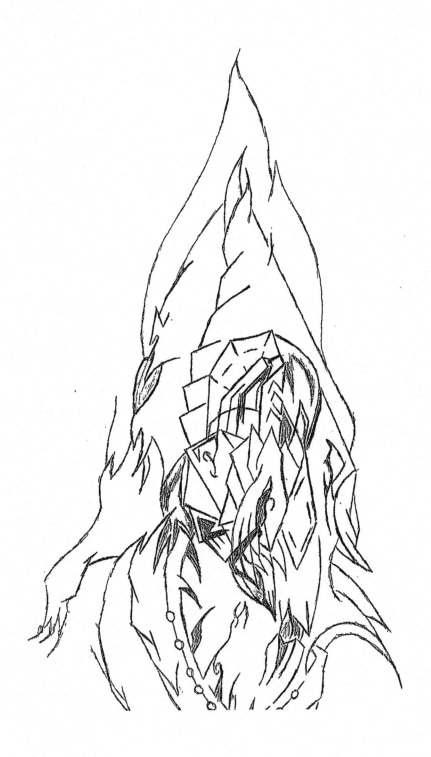

# Shut

How can I look in your eyes
When they're closed?
And how can I understand
What you keep unknown?

Looking at you,
I see the desire within
To trust your heart
And let someone in.

But how can you
With so much pain kept hidden?
All you want is happiness
And the sorrow to be bade good riddance.

## Side Note

Looking in a mirror.

# The Real Me

Don't you see
This mask isn't me?
This isn't who I really am?
But every time I let go,
And the real me I let show,
The look on your face I can't stand.
You look disgusted.
Like I can't even be trusted
As soon as I peel the mask
Because I no longer wear
What you placed there,
And I reveal who I really am.

## Side Note

When you feel that you are being molded and sculpted just so you can be accepted in society.

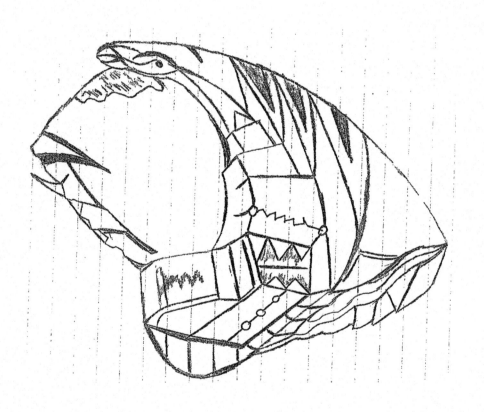

# Twisted

Feeling the pain
While tears run down my face.
Where am I supposed to go?
I can't seem to find my place.

These tears that I cry
Right here in front of you,
Through this wall of darkness,
Are saying the words
That have never been told,
Explaining how much I want to end this.

For every misery
I've created my own fantasy
To hide from the world
When I can't handle reality.
But once you see through me,
You will find
A person who is scared
And tries hard to hide.
For I'm just a girl
Lost in a twirl,
Twisted in nightmares and dreams.
Don't know what's true,
If I can trust you,
Or whether I can even believe.

## Side Note

Tears can really say a lot. Maybe that's why I didn't want to cry in front of people.

# The Cliff

We would climb the hills,
Peaks, and trails
Under the starlit night.
Over the slopes,
Down the valley,
Battling a ferocious fight.
It was fun and games,
Laughs and fears
Until my foot slipped.
But then you grabbed me
And pulled me back up.
As your body leaned and tipped,
You ended up
Being the one to fall
Down the endless pointed cliff.
And I could not believe what I saw:
You, on a bed of rocks,
Poking from your back, which was raw.
I ran desperately down to help you
But found that I could not.
For when I touched your hand,
It felt cold
When it should have been hot.
I can't understand
How in one moment
I am consumed by such a fear,
And now I am left
All alone,
Washing your blood with my tears.

## Side Note

I read a short story in grade 7 or 8, and wrote this piece in an English class. I did the regular assignment as well but wrote this on the side, with my twisted version of the story.

# On the Floor I Cry

On the floor I cry,
Washing away your blood with my tears.
It's not fair,
All the pain you feel
While you try to hide the fear,
But I know it's there.
I feel guilty.
All the love he shows me,
And the pain he gives to you.
I must give you something back.
But all I have is my blood.
Slowly I drop the piece of glass
And watch my blood flow into yours.
Somehow, I think this brings us closer together.
Feeling the pain,
Sadness,
And loneliness,
Having my blood ooze out of my skin,
I create my own bond with you.
Even if it is filled with pain,
I'd rather feel you near me than him.
It's getting late.
It is time for me to go to my room.
I slowly peer in
And see that he is waiting for me.
He holds me,
Kisses me.
I feel so confused.

Why doesn't he treat you like this?
We're in bed now.
Nothing is different.
Our time together has not changed.
Deep down,
I know that what he does to me
He should be doing with you.
You should feel his touch,
His love.
I should be the one feeling pain.
He's done now
And leaves.
In a few moments, your ringing screams will return to my head.
Once again I am left alone,
Washing away your sorrows with my tears,
And drowning your agony with a pool of my blood.

## Side Note

I watched a documentary on a teenage girl and why she was a cutter. She had been abused as a child, and the documentary went into the psychological effects it had on her. I wrote this piece to help people who might have also gone through horrific experiences, whether like this one or different, and let them know writing helps. You'll need an outlet, whether it be drawing, singing, dancing, or running. There are ways that help make the bad memories fade and allow you to try to live again.

# Guilty

You've given me so much love,
And now I can't give it back.
Don't understand what I'm feeling.
Not sure how I should react.
So confused.
Everything's moving so fast.
How much longer
Is this going to last?
Mostly I feel angry,
Although I don't know why.
Because instead of anger,
All I want to do is cry.

## Side Note

I always felt so guilty as a child for how I felt when I had two loving parents and the best big brother ever! Their love is why I am still here today.

# No One Else

You change your words,
Yet your lies stay the same.
I lie in empty darkness,
Where all my fears remain.
Soon I will create
The nightmare that shall come.
As tears roll down my cheeks
And find their way onto my tongue,
Through my lips will pulse
The silence of my scream.
And soon I will awaken
To no one else but me.

## Side Note

When you're still in love with someone who keeps shattering your heart.

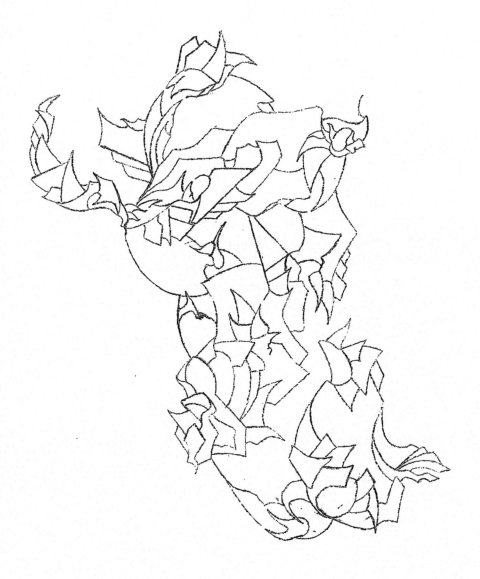

# Bully

Another school, another year.
Another chance to face one's fear.
Another day, another sorrow.
Another lesson that must follow.
One more minute until the hour
In which the bully will make you cower.
One more second in this life
Is all it takes to grab a knife.

Now if only you could turn back time,
Make life into a movie, and hit rewind.
If you could do this, and only then
Could you hit play and start again.
But this isn't a movie; this is real.
And so my blade, you start to feel
Slowly, steadily, sinking in.
And now your blood runs out of your skin.

## Side Note

Every time children are picked on, it brings them that much closer to their breaking points.

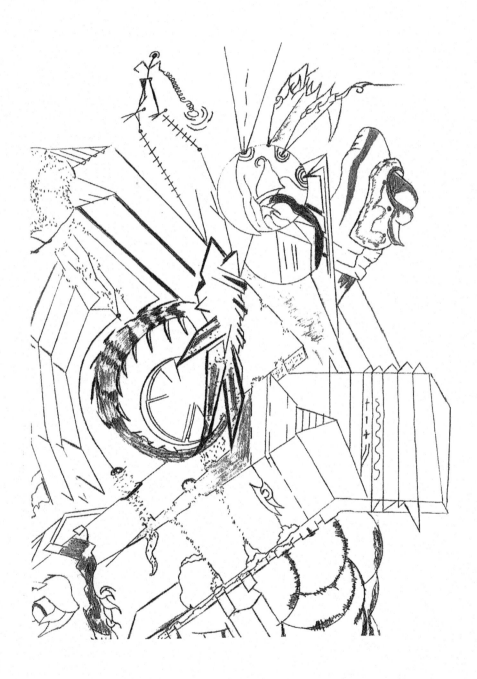

# Life

Wanting to be older
When you're young,
Be able to do everything
That hasn't been done.
Going to new places
That haven't been seen,
And making things real
That you used to dream.

Now you're older,
Wishing you were young,
Thinking about all the things
You wish could be redone.
Now you go to places
That you've already seen,
And now you wonder
Why you no longer dream.

## Side Note

When you take that moment to look back and reflect.

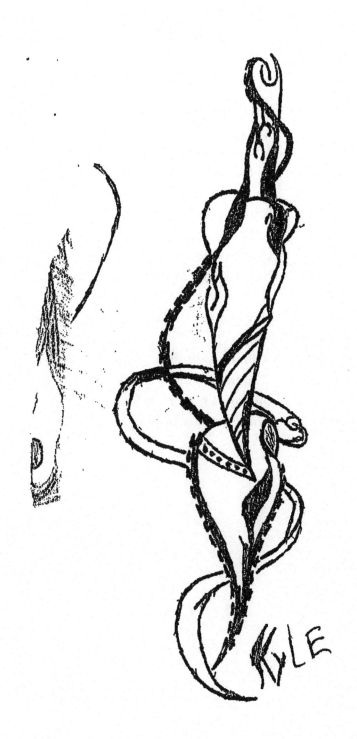

# Empty

Just thinking about
All that I've felt,
And, it saddens me to say,
To feel pain
Or nothing at all.
Which is the better way?

Used to hate crying.
Now I wish I could.
Hated having feelings.
Now I wish I could.

Wanting to be lost,
Wanting to hide;
But now I want to be found.
Am I that hard to find?

## Side Note

When you've managed to shut down, but now you can't seem to start your life back up.

# Gravesight

Wanting to feel love
But only knowing pain,
Wanting to cover up
The blood that now stains
Her soul.
So lost and out of control,
She walks on a path
With no direction to go.

Can't see straight
With a twisted fate.
In search of happiness
Beyond this gate,
She walks on ground
Filled with graves
That lay so sound.
But have these lives been saved?

Each life's
own energy,
Where has it now gone?
If energy cannot be
Created or destroyed,
How can our souls be deployed
To just God or Satan
As our bodies rot
In the ground we lie in?

## Side Note

Again, felt drawn to gravesites, imagining what lives different people might have led.

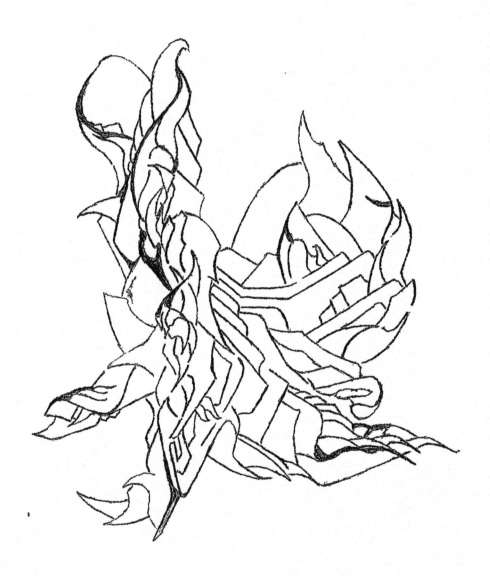

# Un-Chanced

Running so fast
Yet standing still.
Feeling complete,
Needing so much to fulfill.
Comfortable at night,
Scared of day,
Worried what I might do,
Terrified what you might say.
Shaking inside
While holding my ground.
Can't lose
What hasn't been found.

## Side Note

Those teenage years when you're trying to tell yourself that you don't have a crush on someone.

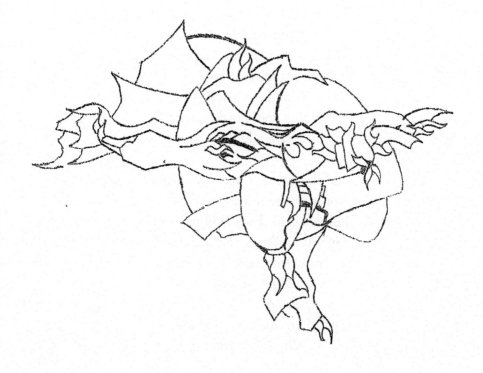

# You Took My Hand

You took my hand
And with it, my heart.
We made each other promise
That nothing could tear us apart.
And it seemed that way.
We were always so happy together.
Try and walk between us.
Our love will guide us through air.
For we were young;
Could never feel old.
Nothing could make us break.
Our love could never go cold.

But fate brought miles between us.
Together again, we could not wait.
But you came back a different man,
And my waiting heart could not understand.
For when you took my hand,
It did not feel the same.
I don't understand.
How did our love fade?
Why isn't it the same?

## Side Note

That first high school sweetheart. You think it's enough to last forever, but a year or two can completely change a person.

# You've Got that Somethin'

You've got that somethin'
That I can't stand.
You take my breath away
When you take my hand.
Looking in your eyes,
What do I find?
That my heart skips a beat
Deep inside.

Oh, won't you take your arms
'N wrap them around me?
Hold me close to you,
But not too tightly.
I wanna
Move around
Next to your body
And have my hands loose
To wander freely.

## Side Note

Boys. They can be fun.

# I Can't Understand

I can't understand.
If you're with the person you want,
How could you want
The heart of another?
How was my heart not enough?
What else did you want me to do?
How could you just walk away?
Why did I even bother?

If my kiss isn't sweet,
If my kinks and kirks aren't neat,
If I'm not beautiful
Enough to keep your eye
As your eyes wandered
And you began to lie.

I can't understand.
If I made you so happy,
How could you be
In the arms of another?
I guess I wasn't enough
To keep you satisfied.
To my heart you lied.
Why did I even bother?

If my kiss isn't sweet,
If my arms you don't need,
If my smile means nothing
Because I mean nothing,
How can you say you love me?
I'd like to demand.
I can't understand.

## Side Note

Every time you give your heart to another, you're giving someone a chance to break it.

# About the Author

Sara .L. Wilson is a new author. Sharing her experiences through poetry, she hopes to help other kids, teens, adults—anyone who may have a mental illness or having a mental breakdown. She knows firsthand the frustrations someone goes through when his or her brain is on "the fritz." The emotional challenges she faced are still being faced today in life, work, and relationships. Fortunately, with love and some life coaching, she has learned key skills that keep her from her breaking points. Most of the time. Not everyone is as lucky. She wrote a couple of poems that were published by The International Society of Poets and JMW Publishing Co. This inspired her to go forward with her poetry, and she wrote this inspiring book of poems to help others.

Dear Kyle, I hope you can see this from Heaven. You told me your dream was to have your artwork in view of the public. We were at the mall, and there was a store filled with paintings. I could see the dream in your eyes before you even said it. I did tell you that it would happen one day.

I hope you have found peace. I knew you were being haunted by your own demons when you drew a picture of a dark cave with a dark figure standing in front. We were hanging out in the apartment I had with a friend. You didn't say much, just drew. All I could do was watch, and to be there for you. It wasn't long after, that the sickness took over full throttle. Next thing I knew you were gone. I just hope you are now free from the monsters inside your head. Hugs. Until I see you again.

CPSIA information can be obtained
at www.ICGtesting.com
Printed in the USA
LVOW13s0825270218
567959LV00001B/1/P